Kingdom of Horses

By

Reham Saadeldin Alsayed Radwan

ISBN:9789779072456

- **Main Characters Of Arabian Horses:**
  1-**Adham:** King of Arabian Horses Kingdom. A charming, slender purebred Arabian horse.
  2-**Ashwaq**: King's wife; a purebred Arabian beautiful mare.
  3- **Baddar**: Son of king Adham; a purebred Arabian horse.
  4-**Jumana:** King's Daughter who is kidnaped by the enemies.
  5-**Abkaar**: Baddar's wife; a purebred Arabian mare.
  6- **Nawwar**: Baddar's son; a small Arabian colt.

- **Main Characters Of Other species of Enemies' Horses:**
  1-**Sakhr**: A plains horse with a big head, long face and tight hooves.
  2- **Saed**: A heavy forest horse; with thick leg hair, it is the origin of the cold-blooded horses.
  3-**Saleet**: a short mountain horse with curly tail hair, he is the origin of lightweight pony.
  4-**Kahlan**: A short pony of Shetland Pony Family, with thick hair and ugly face that looks stupid.
   5- **Nameq**: Sakhr's son, he is of the same family (Plains Horse).

  Note:
  Every horse specie has a similar herd whether for the Arabian horses or other species.

Notes on the story:

The Arabian horse is considered one of the most purebred and expensive species of horses in the world. Arabs have paid attention to preserve the Arabian horse breeds. The Arabian horse is the best specie of horses; he has qualities that distinguish it from other species such as acute intelligence, power, stamina, patience in addition to agility, symmetrical organs, being easy to be leaded and highly motivated.

Allah, the Almighty has honoured Arabian horses and mentioned them in Holy Quran:

"And (He has created) horses, mules, and donkeys, for you to ride and use for show; and He has created (other) things of which you have no knowledge."

Other distinctive features of Arabian horse being exposed to little diseases and recovered fast from injuries, and has great stamina.

The unparalleled courage of the Arabian horse has astonished the whole world; it is not affected by loud sounds but it keeps quiet. Besides, it has fertility that is not decreased by getting older, it is distinguished by being not water-loving as little water is enough for it. The Arabian horse is known for music love and getting delighted with it.

Moreover, zoologists have agreed that Arabian peninsula is the origin of the Arabian horse. This illuminates that the Arabian horse is unparalleled and it is the best specie of horses in the world.

The story is about the conflict between the Arabian horses and other species of horses; the other species attempt to kidnap the Arabian mares in order to improve their breeds because of the fore-mentioned features that characterize the Arabian horse. The king's daughter is kidnaped, and conflicts continue until other species are defeated, the king's daughter is rescued, and the Arabian horses triumph.

Chapter One

On the land of Arabian horses where complete quietness prevails at mid night and all Arabian horses herd is asleep.

While Adham was standing on a rock stargazing at the twinkling stars in the sky, with a calm smile fills his face, his wife Ashwaq came, stood beside him on the rock and smiled at him; both of them expressed their love and affection.

Adham smiled at her expressing his love in the whispering whinny voice.

(Adham and his wife Ashwaq went to Baddar the Arabian horse sleeping on grass.)

Adham and his wife looked at Baddar and gave smile of tenderness and affection.

Ashwaq: "Look, Adham! What beautiful is Baddar…. I hope years pass to see him a brave strong horse."

Adham smiled at his wife, he said: really ….. strong and brave like his father…. I pray God to always protect him and keep any evil far from him.

Ashwaq approached Baddar while he was sleeping to sleep next to him and Adham went to check the herd and get reassured.

In the early morning, on the enemies' land, Sakhr was drinking from a river and was being observed from far by the fool kahlan as he seemed stupid and he came to jolly him as usual. While Sakhr was drinking from the river, Kahlan came closer slowly in order for Sakhr not hear his feet then screamed from his back saying (Buuuuuuuuuuuuuuuuuwa).

Sakhr jumped fast to into the river because he thought that it was a predatory animal. Kahlan laughed and mocked at Sakhr but Sakhr was very furious. He went out of the river, caught a fallen tree branch and hit the fool Kahlan then said: "I do not like your silly humour, IDIOT"

Other friend horses of Sakhr went out; Saed and Saleet whose faces filled with coarseness and cruelty, Saed said very cunningly: "Do you know whom we saw today?!!"

Saleet said:" Adham's wife; the beautiful Ashwaq."

Sakhr got very angry and said to his friends how you have this great chance and you leave it pass without capturing and fetching her to our place.

Saed said, while his face was full with anger, that the situation was tough; Ashwaq was not alone but she was with the Arabian herd and you know well how strong they are, my dear friend.

Sakhr got wrathful with face filled with coarseness, he said :one day I will eliminate Adham and his herd.

On the land of Arabian horses where all small Arabian colts were playing, contesting, laughing and having fun, Baddar was laughing and having fun with them, Adham and his wife were looking smilingly at Baddar.

Then Baddar went up a medium-height hill to look at the kingdom land and Adham went to stand next to him. Baddar was looking happily at the territory and asked Adham: "Is this all wide land is ours, my dad?"

Adham laughed "Yes. my dear, look how charming and fascinating it is. Then, Baddar looked at a far place as it seemed quite barren, he asked about this far land "And this dark spot, is it also ours, daddy?

Adham came near with his head to Baddar and told him very carefully "Do not approach this land in order not to come to any harm, my dear son."

Baddar smiled at his father and went to enjoy himself with his friends in the forest.

Night fell, Adham went to check the herd to get reassured then he moved closer to his wife Ashwaq in so worried whinny voice. She looked at him wondering about the reason behind this worry, she said "Can I know why do you seem so worried?!!!"

Adham answered: Baddar has gone up a hill today and had an incredible curiosity to know about the wasteland existing far, and I know Baddar very well; he is stubborn and incredibly curious about everything.

Ashwaq smiled and said to him "Do not be Afraid, I always watch him from far while he is having fun and playing with his friends, and I will never let him go to any place alone, my dear."

Adham smiled at her expressing his strong love to her and said: "and I will never allow both of you to come to any harm."

In the early morning while birds were singing, sun was shining, all Arabian colts were playing and having fun and all the Arabian horses were looking at their kids with strong tenderness, affection and love.

It remained so until the sun begun to go down and it was naptime, suddenly an injured little Arabian colt screaming out of severe pain entered the Arabian horses land. All Arabian horses have gathered due to this screams and all wondered astonishingly and sympathzingly with this injured colt "what happened?"

Then, the mother of the injured colt came screaming in her whinny voice being worried about her colt, and said very eagerly "what happened, my dear son?!!!" what's wrong with you??!! Answer me my dear little!!"

The little colt was weeping then said "I was attacked and evil Sakhr and his friends were about to kill me but fortunately I managed to flee from those villains miraculously.

The mother got very angry with her colt because he went to this far barren place and told him "why did you go far from you friends??!! Why did you go to this far place without my knowledge??!!"

Adham heard about what happened to this little colt and said angrily " I have warned you all, little colts not to approach this far land, and here you are stubborn little has disobeyed my orders…..!!!"

The little colt felt very ashamed of what he did and asked Adham to forgive and pardon him. He told him with deep regret "love of curiosity made me to go to this far place .. I'm really sorry .. FORGIVE ME PLEASE.. !!

Adham got wrathful and ordered to prevent food from this colt for a whole day as a punishment for what he did and he said angrily " A whole day you will never see food in order to learn the meaning of listening and obeying orders, naughty colt..!!!"

Baddar came close to the injured colt feeling pity for him, he said: "What happened, my dear friend??!!"

The little colt was suffering pain from the injuries and told him " I was about to be killed by the evil Sakhr and his villain friends but I managed to flee miraculously.

The colt looked at the little Arabian colts and told them

"My advice to you is not to approach this far land where Sakhr and his group are: they are evil horses want to destroy us .. Be careful, all my dear friends in order not to get what happened to me..

All the Arabian colts along with Baddar were looking at the injured colt feeling pity for what occurred to him.

Chapter Two

On the following day, while Sakhr was eating grass, Saed and Saleet came to eat and speak with him.

Then Kahlan came with his face full of stupidity, he said to them "Do you remember what happened yesterday, friends … the Arabian colt was about to die but his good luck saved him.

While Saed was eating grass, he seemed angry too. He said "Really… he was about to be perished … I wish I could destroy him..!!"

Sakhr stopped eating; he said angrily "Enough… I do not want to hear more." He went angrily leaving his friends to another way while speaking with himself "how I wished to kill the little colt… I would extremely happy but he was capable of escaping, this little idiot !!!!!!......

Sakhr kept walking on the road before him while his face was full of wrath and followed by Saed and Saleet saying "look, my dear …. Stop being angry."

Sakhr stopped suddenly beside weeds when he found a beautiful Arabian mare was drinking from a river; she got lost while she was with the herd.

All stood behind weeds in complete silence and very carefully. They all said astonishingly and in a low voice, "She is one of the Arabian mares …. How beautiful she is!!"

Everyone was speaking in low voice in order not to be felt by this beautiful mare, suddenly Kahlan came from the back, stupidly spoke in a loud voice. He said "Do not get angry, my friends; days are coming, this chance will be available sooner or later …HaHaHa."

The Arabian mare heard Kahlan's voice, looked at them cautiously and felt danger, then she started running fast.

Sakhr and his friends got angry because of Kahlan's foolishness, Sakhr said wrathfully "What an idiot .. you are really fool."

Sakhr and his friends began running after the mare hopefully to catch her. Sakhr said: "Come on, hurry up, Friends. Do not leave her."

The Arabian mare started running fast followed by Sakhr and his friends; she kept running among hills, plateaus and rocks in loud whinny and behind her are Sakhr and his friends …. Then she reached a big rock bar, all stopped before her and thought that they had the opportunity ….. but the Arabian mare succeeded to jump fast and kick both Sakhr and his friends by the power and courage of the Arabian horse, after that she began running fast to the other road followed by the enemies and Sakhr is saying loudly while he is angry "I will never leave you… I will never let you flee from me…"

Kahlan with face filled with stupidity was watching them all, then the mare came close to a medium-height hill where there was a wooden bridge connecting two hills. Kahlan ran fast to cut the bridge using his teeth, the bridge fell in the gap between the two hills.

The mare came and found the wooden bridge had fallen under the hill …. Kahlan kept laughing and mocking at her; he thought that he was able to defeat her and she would fall in hands of Sakhr and his friends. He laughed sarcastically "HaHaHaHa."

By the intelligence of the Arabian horse, the mare succeeded to jump so high that she could cross the gap between the two plateaus.

Kahlan looked with his face filled with stupidity. Sakhr and his friends came close angrily to see what she did.

After the mare had jumped and crossed the gap, she looked at him sarcastically and said proudly "You know, Sakhr who you are … and who I am … you should know well your worth HaHaHaHa … I am purebred Arab .. you will never defeat us one day .. HaHaHaHa"

The Arabian mare ran to her way with loud whinny spread all over the region.

Sakhr and his friends looked at her wrathfully, he screamed out of rage and said "NOOOO….."

Everyone is full of anger and hit the ground with their hooves.

Kahlan was looking at what happened and foolishly he said:
''Sakhr … I tried to help you but you saw by yourself what happened ..''

Sakhr got angry with him, he said "stop stupidity …,IDIOT"

Sakhr and his friends Saleet and Saed went to high plateau.
Sakhr said: Look at this far land, my friends … It's the land of
Arabian horses"

Saed looked, he said angrily: It does not seem easy as I expected,
we should plan well so that we can obtain an Arabian mare."

Saleet filled with evil told him "really, we should think before
doing anything"

Sakhr was furious, he said "… Yes, it is not such easy .. you
know well the power and goodness of the Arabian horses but we
should obtain a precious treasure whatever it costs."

everyone said evilly "Yes, we will get it sooner or later ..
HaHaHaHa their whinny spread all around."

(There is a difference between their whinny and the Arabian Horses')

Chapter Three

In the early morning, on the land of Arabian horses, Baddar came close to his wounded friend and said "How are you today, my dear??"

The little colt was still exhausted because of the wounds that appeared on him…. Baddar was sympathizing with him in his kind whinny, he wondered "What happened, my dear. Please tell me and how was that?"

The wounded colt remembered, he said; while I was playing and running with my friends, I felt very tired so I sat under a tree and my friends went playing and running until I found myself alone then I started running and looking at hills, rocks, and birds around as I kept away from the ground and sat near to a rock.

The idiot Kahlan went out and I believed him in what he told me; "My dear, I have plenty of delicious sugar.. come with me to eat it together. It is very yummy…!!!"

I went with him and found group of horses which are not of our breed, I was about to die; they started beating me alternately but I managed to escape; It's my good luck.

The colt was telling Baddar what happened while crying strongly but Baddar wondered: " How did you know Kahlan and whom told you his name??!!!"

He kept weeping, he said I heard the enemies calling him.

Baddar asked "How did Kahlan look like???!!!"

The injured colt answered he is short, ugly. And has thick hair…. he really looks ugly!!!

The little colt kept crying, Baddar whinnied sympathzingly and told him "Stop crying and sadness, my dear …….. One day I will take revenge from them and destroy them all … enough .. enough.. crying !!!

In the evening, while everyone was sleeping … Baddar woke up without being felt by anyone then he went to Abkaar the little Arabian mare .. He called out to her in a low voice in order to be heard by no one. He asked her "Abkaar, Are you still asleep??..Abkaar??!!

Abkaar woke up, she astonished and told him what do you want, Baddar. It's late now..!!!!

Baddar and Abkaar went to a high plateau and Baddar said to her "Look at the land of the kingdom how charming it is … you cannot see this beauty except at night: this awesome quietness and bright moonlight ..!!!

Abkaar smiled, whinnied and said "really .. but it has been too late and we should go back otherwise we may be hurt …!!

Baddar laughed at her and said " HaHaHa … What a coward you are!!!

Abkaar prepared herself for going down with Baddar while she was being watched from far by a black cheetah with fierce features and vicious and frightening yellow eyes; It seemed hungry.

The cheetah was about to pounce on them but Abkaar screamed strongly and Baddar whinnied loudly ……

They ran and the hungry cheetah ran after them, they had jumped before he pounced on them, then Adham and two friends of the Arabian horses appeared; he hit the cheetah so strongly that he fell on the ground …. and escaped. Baddar and Bakaar seemed so ashamed of what happened, Adham spoke full of rage, he said " In the morning we will meet …… come on."

In the early morning, the Arabian horses were gathering and speaking about what Baddar has done and how he would risk the life of his cousin Abkaar; the little mare.

Baddar was standing with his mother Ashwaq deeply ashamed of what happened, she said: "Go to your father, Baddar. Excuse for what happened ..; Adham is so furious..!!"

Baddar went to his father to excuse and he was angry. Adham said wrathfully "How dare you to leave the herd at such late time of night, and the worst is to risk your cousin Abkaar's life!!!"

Baddar excused and he would never do this again. He said "I am sorry, I promise you this will never happen again..!!"

Adham was still angry, he told him "Go now with the friends."

Baddar went to play with the friends while Adham was looking at him and his face is still full of anger.

Ashwaq came close to him sympathzingly she said: "Do not worry, my dear, Tomorrow Baddar will be unparalleled strong and brave …

Adham smiled at her … and approached her by head showing his strong tenderness and love to his wife..!!

Chapter Four

In the early morning, on the land of enemies, all horses were eating grass and Kahlan also was eating grass with the herd.

Kahlan noticed from a distance a female of his Family; Shetland Pony. She exactly looked like him; he approached her to express his admiration of her. He said "Good morning, beautiful … Can I know your name??"

The mare was eating grass alone when she found Kahlan admiring her, she looked at him with dissatisfaction then left him and went to another place.

Kahlan went after her and he was still talking to her and admiring her. He said: "why do not you answer me, my dear ..??"

She seemed angry and screamed in his face. She said "Go away, idiot otherwise I will give you unforgettable lesson."

Kahlan mocked at her and started laughing "HaHaHa"

Suddenly, a horse of Sakhr's family appeared and hit Kahlan until he fell on the ground. He said "Do not approach her again otherwise I will destroy you, idiot."

The mare laughed at Kahlan's foolishness and went with her Shetland Pony herd.

At night, both Saed and Saleet met, they laughed loudly when Kahlan told them what happened to him this morning and how he got ashamed of what a horse of Sakhr's family did with him in front of a Shetland pony female.

Kahlan was irritated of what happened; Saed and Saleet were mocking and laughing at him for what he had done with the female who belonged to his family and the punishment he deserved.

Kahlan went and left them still laughing. Sakhr came; he seemed irritated. He said "This laughing is enough."

Saed replied sarcastically "You do not know what happened to Kahlan in the morning" but Sakhr was still angry and said to them "I do not want to hear anything it's late and we should wake up early; the herd needs food ….

So, everyone left … to receive a new day.

On the land of Arabian horses, in the early morning while the sun is bright .. Adham was eating some apples that fell from a tree.

Baddar approached him with his face full of shame and he was sorry for what happened.

Adham approached by his head to Baddar and said "Listen well to what I will say, my son .. You are still young … you should know and understand well what I am saying .. do not go to any place alone .. Did you hear what I said? .. do not risk your life and the other's.

Baddar was feeling very sorry and promised his father not to do this again. Adham smiled at him. He said "So, go now and play with friends."

Baddar went to play and have fun with his friends.

Ashwaq was looking at them from far while she was smiling at them.

When Baddar went to play with friends .. Ashwaq approached her husband Adham and both were expressing their love in whinny.

Adham and Ashwaq went to the forest laughing, having fun and expressing their love.

Adham and Ashwaq stood in front of a river .. Kahlan the idiot was standing between trees peeping .. he saw Adham and his wife with him.

Kahlan called out quietly to both Saed and Saleet "Come, Guys .. Look! Who are there?"

Both Saed and Saleet came and found Adham and his wife .. and everyone said "Yes, it's Adham's wife .. it's really a beautiful Arabian mare .."

Sakhr came from their back to look while his face was full of evil; he found Ashwaq: Adham's wife and how much he wished to be his wife in order to have a generation characterized by power and solidity like the Arabian horse.

Days and years passed, Baddar had three years and became a slender beautiful Arabian horse.

While Baddar was with his friends: the other Arabian horses as they all became beautiful Arabian horses …., Adham came calling out to Baddar who was standing with his cousin Abkaar who also became a beautiful Arabian mare.

Adham was calling out " Baddar … Abkaar … come with me and look!"

Baddar and Abkaar came as Adham the king was calling out to them and they had passion and love of curiosity repeating "we wonder … what does he want?"

The surprise was that Ashwaq gave birth to a beautiful little mare.

Baddar and Abkaar were happy and said "what's her name?? she is really beautiful .. …..!!!

Adham replied "Jumana"

Everyone was pleased with the little newborn.

Days passed, Jumana became in her first year and she was playing and having fun with friends, Ashwaq was looking at her with mother's affection.

Ashwaq came close to her daughter while she was playing and having fun with friends and said: "Jumana, this is enough … let's go"

Jumana came to her mother laughing and said: "Mum, I feel so thirsty."

Ashwaq and Jumana went to a river; Ashwaq was drinking and behind her Jumana. While Ashwaq and Jumana were on a river, one beautiful butterfly came on a flower near to Jumana.

Jumana looked at her, she smiled at the beautiful butterfly and tried to jolly, the butterfly flied and Jumana ran after her smiling and laughing, she said: "Come, beautiful butterfly …..HaHa .. I was about to catch you, come to me Where you are going? HaHaHa …."

Chapter Five

Jumana started running after the butterfly while she was having fun, playing with her, laughing and trying to catch her … but the butterfly was getting higher and higher to the hill surrounded.

Jumana got lost after she had run after the butterfly … she went out of the spot of the Arabian herd.

Suddenly, Sakhr, Saed and Saleet appeared before Jumana while they seemed vicious. They said to her "Where are you going, little beautiful ..!!! HaHaHa,

Do you like our land ..???!! HaHaHa

Jumana seemed terrified because she felt that the situation is not in her favour and begun running, asking for help and said: "HELP ….. DAD .. MUM ….)"

Jumana ran while she was screaming and behind her are the enemies,Sakhr said: "I will never leave you ….. you can never escape from me …."

Ashwaq felt that there was a danger …; she turned back and did not find her daughter Jumana. Ashwaq started running fast searching for Jumana. Ashwaq's whinny raised and started calling out "Jumana …Jumana … Jumana …. Where are you, my dear……??!!"

Ashwaq started running everywhere.. until she went away from Arabian Horses' land.

Ashwaq heard Jumana's screams while she was asking for help and kept running searching for her. Suddenly, the vicious Sakhr appeared before her with his face full of anger and evil, then Ashwaq said to him wrathfully "Where is my daughter .. Where is my daughter, wretch.. minor….. ?????

Sakhr kept standing before her and trying approach her … Ashwaq moved backwards while saying … Go away, idiot otherwise I will destroy you ….. I I will give you a lesson you will never forget …… GO AWAY.

Sakhr mocked at her and laughed …… HaHaHaHa … HaHaHa

Suddenly, Ashwaq saw her daughter with the enemies above a plateau while she was screaming and asking for help. She Said "HELP …HELP .. MUM ….. PLEASE DO NOT LEAVE ME ALONE WITH THESE VILLAINS"

Ashwaq tried to rescue her only daughter Jumana .. but she saw Sakhr in front of her and Saed and Saleet behind her. Everyone has surrounded her so that she could not move.

Sakhr and Saleet hit her; she fell down on the ground.

Jumana screamed out of the horror of this scene ….. she was crying .. "MUM…MUM… NO NO MUM…"

Ashwaq remained lying on the ground pretending being affected by falling on the ground, then by the Arabian horse's intelligence, she jumped and hit strongly by her legs Sakhr, Saed, and Saleet and started running fast and her whinny spread all over the place.

Ashwaq started running fast and behind her Sakhr, Saleet and Saed whose faces were full of evil, Sakhr changed his direction, Saed and Saleet were still behind her. Suddenly, Ashwaq found Sakhr before her again.

Ashwaq did not find another road except the side road: it was high and leaded to a high plateau.

Sakhr ran after her with face was full of evil and told his friends .. "Leave her …. Leave her to me … I will handle her …… HaHaHa"

Consequently, Ashwaq reached the top of the high plateau and did not find another road, Sakhr stood before her and exchanged looks of challenge and strong hatred.

She tried to hit Sakhr but he moved backwards. Suddenly, he hit Ashwaq by his legs so Ashwaq fell down the plateau.

Jumana watched what happened to Ashwaq while she was screaming; "MUM .. MUM .. MUM … NO NO NO NO"

Consequently, Ashwaq fell down the high plateau, it was the tragic end for her as she hit the ground and she was still breathing her last ….

Jumana was still crying out of the horror of the situation "NO…. NO…NO…MUM"

Chapter Six

Sun started to go gown, Ashwaq and Jumana did not appear .. Adham was standing and seemed worried …. He said "I wonder where are you, Ashwaq … where are you, Jumana ….. I hope you are fine … why is this worrying lateness…??!!"

Baddar came to his father while he was worried about his sister Jumana and his mother Ashwaq. Adham smiled at him, he told him "Do not worry, my dear …. I will go and search for them …… they might have got lost … my dear, wait here … I will search for them after a while."

Adham remained standing and looking at the sky … and at the surroundings while he seemed worried.. "I wonder where are you, Ashwaq?!!! Where are you, Jumana ….???!!"

Night fell but Ashwaq and Jumana did not appear .. they did not leave any trace.

Adham was still worried about them. He said "I can not wait more than this, I will go and search for Ashwaq and Jumana.

Baddar came with his father. He said neither am I, dad .. I will go with you …. I will search for my mum and sister .. I can not wait …"

Adham and Baddar started searching for Ashwaq and Jumana everywhere; they were calling out to Ashwaq and Jumana "Ashwaq ..Ashwaq ..- Jumana …Jumana"

Baddar was calling out "MUM …MUM… WHERE ARE YOU, JUMANA…??

Suddenly, a lioness roared seeking food to eat. Baddar seemed quite worried.. but Adham was still firm, he wanted to find her wife and daughter.

He told Baddar "If you are afraid …Go … Go back … for me …. I will never return till I find Ashwaq and Jumana."

The lioness appeared suddenly before Adham and Baddar, she was hungry …. Adham and Baddar ran and the lioness after them she wanted to attack them.

Adham changed his route to the opposite road .. while the lioness remained running and running after Baddar. Adham reached a high rock above a little hill while the lioness kept running after Baddar.. by the intelligence of the Arabian horse, Adham bravely pushed the rock until fell on the lioness .. Adham succeeded to rescue himself and Baddar .. from this predatory lioness.

They began running searching for Ashwaq and Jumana ..with their loud whinny that spread everywhere …..

After that, Both Adham and Baddar continued searching for Ashwaq and Jumana. Suddenly, Adham heard a low voice seemed asking for help next to a river; It was Ashwaq calling out while she was breathing her last … Adham .. Adham .. I am here …. Come.

Adham and Baddar turned to the voice source and surprisingly ….. Ashwaq seemed breathing her last.

Adham and Baddar approached her while Adham's face seemed very worried. Adham told her astonishingly "Ashwaq, what is this? ..and what happened??!! …. Who did so with you …??!!!"

Baddar said wonderingly and astonishingly for this sad situation "MUM.. MUM … WHAT'S WRONG WITH YOU? WHO DID SO WITH YOU???!!!

Ashwaq was breathing her last, she said to Adham "Do not care about me, my dear .. but Jumana .. Take care of her .. Sakhr and the villains took her … PLEASE RESCUE MY DAUGHTER …… PLEASE ADHAM."

Consequently, Ashwaq died ….. Baddar started crying about his mum " NO..NO.. DO NOT LEAVE ME MUM"

Adham's eyes shed tears.

In the early morning, Adham was standing alone on the land of Arabian horses while his face was full of sadness and all the Arabian horses were sad because of what happened to Ashwaq.

After that, Baddar came close to his father while his eyes was still shedding tears and his face was full of sadness, then Adham gave angrily a whinny spread all over the place in order to meet with the Arabian herd , he told them in very strength and challenge

"Listen well, friends; Sakhr and his group are villains and they will never leave us…"

"We should destroy them before they destroy us and take our females …. Eliminate us .. and our purebred breed…"

The horses whinnied loudly, strongly and challengingly.. expressing strength and courage to revenge from these villains.

Adman whinnied loudly … with strength and challenge, he said "I will never leave you Sakhr … I will revenge from you ….. Sooner or later ……"

Whinny was still spreading all over the place.

Accordingly, Jumana became captive on the land of enemies; she was still in her first year … she was still little Arabian mare.

One day, on the enemies land, Jumana was standing under the shadow of a tree, she seemed melancholy.

The villain Sakhr came close to her trying to infuriate her ……. "How are you today, my dear???

Jumana got angry and approached the river and managed to make some drops of river water fall on his face by her legs, she said:

"Go away, villain….!!"

Saleet, Saed and Kahlan laughed at Sakhr.

Sakhr got angry and started hitting Jumana, she fell on the ground crying ….. Everyone was laughing at her when she fell down…

Then, she said to them while she was crying: "One day my dad will come and revenge from you all.. idiots….!!

Everyone was still laughing and mocking at her.

Chapter Seven

Days and Years passed, Baddar became three years; he was slender and beautiful with all the features of the purebred Arabian horses.

Baddar was standing alone full of Sadness and melancholy, Abkaar noticed this sadness, she turned to him; she knew the reason for his sorrow.

Abkaar told him "Enough of this sorrow, my dear …… years passed; this unfortunate event ….. Should be in limbo"

Baddar got angry with Abkaar because of what she said, he told her very angrily "What…!! What are you saying…?!! My mum was killed and my sister was kidnapped, One day you may be a victim …. Then you say limbo…!! How dare you …??!!

Then, Baddar left her while he was furious about what she said.

Baddar left his wife Abkaar and went running in the forest among hills, mountains, and rocks; he got a kind of nervous turmoil ….

Poor Baddar, he felt severe pain due to his mother's death and his sister's kidnapping. He kept running while his eyes were shedding tears .. then he stopped next to a river and his face was full of sadness.

Kahlan appeared from his back , he said, "What makes you cry, my little dear?"

Baddar turned back, he got angry with Kahlan, hit him and said "Go away, idiot…."

Kahlan fell down on the ground. Baddar came close to him; he put his legs on Kahlan's neck, wrathfully he said: "Who killed my mum??!! Speak or I will you, idiot..!!.....

Kahlan was afraid of Baddar's strength, he said:

"Leave me… I did not kill her … believe me …. Sakhr is the one who killed her … and took her daughter …. Please, leave me … leave me alone …HELP …I am almost out of breath .. PLEASE.

Baddar got so angry when he heard Kahlan's words… Kahlan had escaped.

Baddar remained standing alone in the forest …… sad for what happened.

It became late, Adham and Abkaar were waiting Baddar; they seemed very worried.

Abkaar Said: "Baddar has been late, uncle …I fear that something bad happened to him..; he left me while he was angry….!!!

Adham went to search for Baddar among rocks, hills, trees and everywhere in the forest, it was a rainy day…..

Adham kept searching for Baddar until he felt so tired; he sat to rest next to a river.

Baddar went out from a tree side, he came close and said in a sad and low voice …. "Dad ……!!!"

Adham said: "Where were you …..??!! I was so worried about you .. all the herd was so worried ….!!!"

Baddar said sadly I was searching for my sister Jumana .. Do you know who killed my mum, dad?..... It's Sakhr .. Sakhr …the wicked Sakhr …!!!

Adham got surprised of what he heard, he said "and how did you know that….??!!"

Baddar said "I saw that idiot Kahlan and threatened him to kill if he did not tell me the truth …. Here I knew everything …….."

Adham got furious, he said:

"I will never rest until I revenge from the villain Sakhr….One day I will revenge from him this villain and all the enemies…… One day I will meet the wicked Sakhr."

In the morning, Abkaar was awaiting Adham and Baddar…. Baddar came

while Abkaar was awaiting him so eagerly, she was sorry for what she said.

She ran towards Baddar and said: "Forgive me, my dear …..you are right .. we all are with you .. and we will search for Jumana until we find her and revenge from the enemies … I did not mean it PLEASE FORGIVE ME…!!"

Baddar and Adham smiled at her, the Arabian horses' whinny raised and spread all over the place to express strength and courage.

Chapter Eight

Days passed until Jumana became a beautiful mare while she was captive in the enemies' land.

Jumana was standing beside a tree, Nameq tried to approach her, "Why are you always angry, my dear…??!!?" He said to her.

She looked at him very angrily, hit him strongly and said: "Go away, idiot……!!!"

The idiot Kahlan laughed at this situation, Nameq got angry and said to her "You are arrogant, One day I will give you a lesson, arrogant."

Nameq went to his father Sakhr while his face was full of rage, he told him "I am sick of this stubborn, Dad……"

Sakhr looked at him, he said "Do not worry, my dear son; she is in our land and cannot escape, she is in our land; she will be for you sooner or later and we will reproduce the best generation …. The purebred.. the original.. HaHaHa…"

Everyone laughed and raised their whinny…… Nameq got pleased with his father's promise.

Jumana was standing far while her face was full of sadness; she remembered what happened to her beautiful mother Ashwaq.

Days passed, Baddar became a slender youth; he married Abkaar and had Nawwar; a beautiful little Arabian colt.

Adham was standing on a rock while his face was full of anger when Baddar approached him; he said "Enough sadness, my dear father"

Adham looked sadly at him, he said "Years passed, my dear son .. until now we do not know where is Jumana…?and what happened to her…??!! But I am sure she is alive…

Baddar smiled at him, he said "Do not worry my dear, I will find Jumana sooner or later, I will never give up the matter easily …… I will destroy the enemies ……. Do not worry, my dear. We will find Jumana ……."

Adham smiled at him then he went to his grandson Nawwar to have fun with him, Baddar and Abkaar were looking at them in love and affection.

At night, On the land of enemies; everyone was asleep "kh …khkhkhkh…khkhkhkhkh…."

Jumana woke up quietly trying to escape; she passed by the enemies horses while they were asleep.

She passed by Kahlan while he was disturbingly snoring: "khkhkhkhkhkh …khkhkhkhkh……khkhkhkhkh"

Kahlan opened his eyes very maliciously pretending that he was still asleep. Then, Jumana started running fast attempting to go out of the enemies' land.

Jumana kept running fast but Sakhr surprised her and stood in front of her while he appeared evil. Then, she changed her direction but she found Saleet in one side and Saed in the other side.

Everyone laughed, Sakhr said very sarcastically "It's not such easy, my dear….. Do not think about escape again … or I will give you a lesson you will never forget for your whole life"… "HaHaHa…."

Everyone laughed sarcastically ……

"HaHaHa……..HaHaHa"

She went with them against her will to the enemies' land.

What a poor; she could not escape …. She started crying so hard.

In the early morning, on the Arabian horses' land, Nawwar was playing and having fun with the friends as usual, both Baddar and Abkaar were looking at her son while he was enjoying himself and playing.

Adham came close to them, he said "Good morning, my lovers.."

Abkaar looked at him then Baddar turned to him, he said "Good morning, my dear dad…… how are you today??!!!"

Adham smiled and said "I am fine. Thanks God …. But where is my dear Nawwar??!!..."

Abkaar smiled, she said "he is having fun with the friends as usual."

Adham looked at Nawwar and screamed: "Nawwar.. Nawwar…….Be careful"

He started running fast towards Nawwar; there was a snake behind Nawwar, she was about to attack Nawwar with her poisonous teeth …

Adham started running fast towards the snake…. He fell upon the snake and hit her by his strong feet, he repeated that on the snake's head until it was smashed and she died.

Both Baddar and Abkaar were running to see what happened, Abkaar said with the mother's affection "My son.. What's wrong with you?!!! Are you okay……?!!!!

Nawwar told her very innocently "Do not worry my dear mum, I am fine .. thanks to my lovely grandpa, he rescues my life .. how much I wish to become as brave and strong as my grandpa ..Baddar smiled, he said "you are still young, my dear…."

Adham laughed, he said "HaHaHa…. Courage and strength are not such easy and they will not bear fruit except after you face this hard life, my dear.

Everyone laughed, Nawwar said "So….let's go my grandpa …. I want to learn from you…"

Adham smiled and went to have fun with his grandson Nawwar in the forest.

Adham and Nawwar went to the forest to enjoy themselves, play with each other and laugh; Adham was competing his grandson and running cheerfully.

Then, Nawwar stood on a high rock and looked at this far barren place. Adham wondered "Where are you Nawwar…..???!!"

Adham found his grandson look at that place, he stood beside him and said "What's wrong with you, Nawwar??!!! What are you looking at……????!!!"

Nawwar said: "I asked my dad about this place and he never answered me…and I really want to know what this place is, my; dear grandpa…. And why it seems barren and lifeless …….????…. I am sure you know well…….."

Adham seemed very sad and remembered what happed to his family , in a sad voice he told him "Listen well, my dear son …… Arabian horses are unparalleled all over the world.. We are the symbol of power and courage … Stamina and patience …."

Then, he said, my dear, on this barren far land there are a group of villain horses, they do not belong to us at all but they want to destroy us totally.

Nawwar astonished, he said "Are they also Arabian horses …..??!!!!"

Adham answered "No, my dear … they are not absolutely Arabian horses... this barren land is full of wicked therefore do not go there alone….

Nawwar looked at him wondering "why ……???!!!"

Adham continued: on this land there are horses called plains horses; they are short, have wide lines on legs … also there are the forest horses which are the origin of all cold-blooded horses.. like the idiot Kahlan: short and ugly …. There is no beauty except the beauty of the Arabian horses ….. Did you get it?

Therefore, do not go to this place alone, my dear, you may come to harm … as you know these villains want to destroy us .. because of our charming qualities which are not in any horses on earth..

Adham smiled at him, he said "I wish you understood the lesson well ….. my dear."

Nawwar smiled, he said "yes, my grandpa …… I understood now…."

Adham and Nawwar started to move to their land and the herd ……

Chapter Nine

At quiet and silent night, Jumana was standing sad and speaking with herself: "I wonder ….. what is your destiny, Jumana …?!!! Until now no one came to rescue you …..!!!.

Now I have two years and became old and captive …. Where are you my dad to rescue me from these villains ……???!!

Sakhr came from her behind laughing at her "HaHaHaHa ……your destiny is with Sakhr and his friends, my dear. Tomorrow you will be the happiest wife and give birth to our dear sons …. The most purebred breed .. HaHaHa…..

Jumana got angry with him, she said: "Go away, villain…..."

Sakhr laughed strongly, he said "Do you think you can escape … HaHaHa …… what naïve you are ……"

She looked at him angrily "One day you will pay the price for all what you do, villain killer …!!!

Sakhr left her while he was laughing at her …. But her face was full of sadness.

In the early morning, on the Arabian horses' land, Adham was standing and looking at his grandson Nawwar while he was playing and having fun with the friends but Adham seemed very sad; he still remembered his wife and his lost daughter.

Baddar came and looked at Nawwar, next to him was his wife Abkaar , she said "look, Baddar …. Nawwar seems happy while he is having fun with the friends ….."

Baddar was silent a little then said very intelligently …

"Yes, Nawwar is the bait that helps us to destroy the enemies."

Abkaar astonished of what Baddar said, she said "What …….??! What did you say …..?! Nawwar ….. Nawwar …… Are you serious …?! ……Or something went wrong with your brain …!!! …."

Baddar looked at her angrily, he said "I am serious, Abkaar …. And I am very aware of what I am saying……"

Abkaar got angry; she said to him "Listen to me well, we are really sorry for what happened to your mother and Jumana …. But this does not mean to risk Nawwar's life …. Do you understand me….?!!

Baddar looked at her wrathfully. He said "Nawwar is not only your son ….he is also my son … and I fear to do harm to him …….. Do not be afraid … Do not be afraid, my dear …. Do you understand he is not your son alone ……!!!!

On the enemies' land, Nameq is trying to rape Jumana. He laughed sarcastically …. "HaHaHa … come, beautiful …… HaHa"

She was running out of fear of him while everyone was laughing at this scene; it was Jumana and Nameq's wedding and all the horses were laughing and mocking at Jumana while she was resisting with all her power.

Meanwhile, the Arabian horses were ready to execute the plan….. while Abkaar was standing far in the forest watching the situation and a group of the Arabian herd was having fun and playing….. with them Nawwar: everyone was playing and having fun …. The other Arabian horses were hidden behind rocks, trees, and hills to execute Baddar's plan …….

The malicious Kahlan watched that, he said "A new victim… I should tell Sakhr rapidly before they escape …… HaHaHa"

He went fast to tell Sakhr and his friends ……. He said: "My friends, I saw a group of Arabian horses while their females were laughing and enjoy themselves near our land.. It is a good chance for us …".

Soon Sakhr, Saed and Saleet came ….

Saed and Saleet looked at the little mares; the little mares screamed out of fear, Saed said .. "Take Care of these kids, Saleet …. I will take care of this beautiful mare …. To become also from our females …….. come on .. come on…

Abkaar started running fast to escape from the enemies and Saleet was behind her. She was running very strongly and her whinny spread all over the place ……..

Sakhr came before her while his face was full of evil …. Abkaar found Saed behind and Sakhr behind her ….. she started running in a side road but she found another group of enemies belonging to Saed, Saleet, and Sakhr's family … Abkaar became surrounded from all sides.

Sakhr laughed sarcastically, he said "HaHaHaHaHa ……. This is the end of every stubborn …. Go to your destiny with Jumana …HaHaHaHa …."

The Arabian horses were with them watching what happened to Abkaar; Adam was hidden as well as Baddar …. Abkaar was driven to the enemies' land, the Arabian horses were watching that to execute the plan ……… so that they can know the place of lost Jumana …

Consequently, Abkaar reached the enemies' land while she was surrounded as a captive also … Jumana was running and screaming asking for help while Nameq was running after her …… saying "Come, my beautiful.. HaHaHa….."

Suddenly, the Arabian horses appeared and surrounded the whole enemies' place. It was so great force whose whinny filled the whole place that put horror and fear into the enemies' heart ….

Abkaar laughed …she said .. "HaHaHaHa ……. What idiot you are, Sakhr? .. HaHaHaHa"

The clash took place; the Arabian horses attacked the other species of horses. Baddar and Adham stood looking at Sakhr with strong desire to revenge from him ... Sakhr got scared and began running while Baddar and Adam were behind him …. Adham told Baddar …. Leave him to me, Baddar; today is my best day…. This is my only chance ….

Sakhr began running and Adham was behind him running fast and strongly with desire to revenge from him. While Sakhr was escaping from Adham, he went up the same place where Ashwaq went. Adham was behind him with strong insistence, Sakhr found there was no way before him, Adham approached him while his face was full of desire of revenge …. He said to him "Today is your day, villain killer … Adham hit him very strongly with deep revenge whinny .. Sakhr fell down … then died, Adham managed to revenge for his wife in the same way that Sakhr killed Ashwaq.

Adham looked from the top of the hill at Jumana and he Knew that she was his daughter; she looked like her wife Ashwaq, he ran towards her while calling out "My daughter Jumana ……. My dear……." Jumana started running saying "Dad …… Dad ……Dad"

Consequently, it was a warm meeting between Adham and his daughter Jumana after years …. He succeeded to rescue his daughter from the enemies … Baddar came close to his sister, he said "Jumana … my dear sister.."

It was a meeting full of warm feelings …. Finally, the Arabian horses managed to defeat the enemies who fled when the Arabian horses herd attacked with their whinny that filled all over the place.

This illuminates that Arabian horses are unparalleled in the world; they got the attention of the foreign orientalists. Arabs used to preserve the Arabian horse breeds; the Bedouin man refused completely to intermingle his mare with a horse of another specie to preserve the Arabian horse. From some previous scenes, we find the intelligence of the Arabian horse, his purebred, power, stamina, fertility …. That's why the enemies wished to improve their breeds.